EASY READERS

Dear Parent:

Congratulations! Your child is taking the first steps on an exciting journey. The destination? Independent reading!

STEP INTO READING® will help your child get there. The program offers five steps to reading success. Each step includes fun stories and colorful art. There are also Step into Reading Sticker Books, Step into Reading Math Readers, Step into Reading Phonics Readers, Step into Reading Write-In Readers, and Step into Reading Phonics Boxed Sets—a complete literacy program with something to interest every child.

Learning to Read, Step by Step!

Ready to Read   Preschool–Kindergarten
• big type and easy words • rhyme and rhythm • picture clues
For children who know the alphabet and are eager to begin reading.

Reading with Help   Preschool–Grade 1
• basic vocabulary • short sentences • simple stories
For children who recognize familiar words and sound out new words with help.

Reading on Your Own   Grades 1–3
• engaging characters • easy-to-follow plots • popular topics
For children who are ready to read on their own.

Reading Paragraphs   Grades 2–3
• challenging vocabulary • short paragraphs • exciting stories
For newly independent readers who read simple sentences with confidence.

Ready for Chapters   Grades 2–4
• chapters • longer paragraphs • full-color art
For children who want to take the plunge into chapter books but still like colorful pictures.

STEP INTO READING® is designed to give every child a successful reading experience. The grade levels are only guides. Children can progress through the steps at their own speed, developing confidence in their reading, no matter what their grade.

Remember, a lifetime love of reading starts with a single step!

For Richard John Gagliano, Jr.
—C. W.

Published in the United States by Random House Children's Books, a division of Random House, Inc., 1745 Broadway, New York, NY 10019, and in Canada by Random House of Canada Limited, Toronto.

Step into Reading, Random House, and the Random House colophon are registered trademarks of Random House, Inc.

Visit us on the Web!
StepIntoReading.com
www.randomhouse.com/kids
www.barbie.com

Educators and librarians, for a variety of teaching tools, visit us at
www.randomhouse.com/teachers

ISBN: 978-0-375-86839-9 (trade) — ISBN: 978-0-375-96839-6 (lib. bdg.)

Printed in the United States of America   10 9 8 7 6 5 4 3 2 1

Barbie i can be...

A Ballerina

By Christy Webster

Illustrated by Kellee Riley

Random House 🏠 New York

Barbie loves to dance.
Today she has
ballet class.

Barbie and Teresa
take ballet together.

The girls practice
the positions.

6

First, second, third, fourth, and fifth.

Barbie leaps
across the room.

Teresa stands

on her toes.

Barbie and Teresa
want to be ballerinas
in a ballet company.

A ballet company
is a group
of ballet dancers.
Dancing is their job!

The teacher invites
Barbie and Teresa
to meet a real ballerina.

The next day,
Barbie and Teresa
visit the City Ballet.

They meet Becca.
She is a ballerina
in the City Ballet.

Barbie and Teresa
spend the day
with her.

They go
to the dressing room.
Becca shows them
her locker.

The girls put on
their ballet shoes.

Becca takes
Barbie and Teresa
to ballet class.

They meet
the other dancers.
Barbie and Teresa
join the class.

First,
they stretch.
The dancers stand
at the barre.

They point their toes
to the front, side,
and back.

They move their arms
up and down.

The dancers
take turns leaping.
The teacher watches.
The class is like
Barbie and Teresa's
class.

After lunch,
the dancers practice
for their show.
They practice
on the stage.

They dance
the same steps
over and over.

Becca is the star!

She practices her solo.

The director needs
two more dancers.

Barbie and Teresa
will play small parts
in the ballet!

Becca teaches
Barbie and Teresa
the steps.

Then they put
on their costumes.

It is time for
the show!
Barbie and Teresa
can be ballerinas!